Rudie Nudie

To Izzy, Charli, Cat and The Bundles

The ABC 'Wave' device and the 'ABC KIDS' device are
trademarks of the Australian Broadcasting Corporation and
are used under licence by HarperCollins*Publishers* Australia.

First published in Australia in 2011
This edition published in 2012
by HarperCollins*Children'sBooks*
a division of HarperCollins*Publishers* Australia Pty Limited
ABN 36 009 913 517
harpercollins.com.au

Copyright © Emma Quay 2011

emmaquay.com

The right of Emma Quay to be identified as the author and
illustrator of this work has been asserted by her in accordance
with the *Copyright Amendment (Moral Rights) Act 2000.*

HarperCollins*Publishers*
Level 13, 201 Elizabeth Street, Sydney NSW 2000, Australia
Unit D1, 63 Apollo Drive, Rosedale, Auckland 0632, New Zealand

National Library of Australia Cataloguing-in-Publication entry:

Quay, Emma.
    Rudie nudie / Emma Quay.
    ISBN: 978 0 7333 3173 2 (pbk.)
    For pre-school age.
    Australian Broadcasting Corporation.
A823.3

Designed and typeset by Ellie Exarchos
Emma Quay used pencil, paper
 and Photoshop for the illustrations
Colour reproduction by Graphic Print Group, Adelaide
Printed and bound in China by RR Donnelley on
 157gsm Chinese Gold East Matt Art

11 10 9 8   16 17 18 19

Rudie Nudie

story and pictures by
Emma Quay

ABC
Books

One, two Rudie Nudie,
Rudie Nudie in the bath.

Squeaky clean and splishing, splashing, sploshing—

Rudie Nudie laugh.

Rudie Nudie
bye-bye bubbles.

Rudie Nudie dripping wet.

Dancing footprints on the bathmat,

Rudie Nudie pirouette.

Rudie hugged up in a bundle.
Rudie Nudie on the floor.

Rolling over,

jumping up,

and Rudie Nudie out the door.

Rudie all along the floorboards.

Rudie Nudie on the rug.

Tiptoe
quickstep
on the
doormat,

Rudie Nudie
nice and snug.

Rudie roly-poly tumbles.

Rudie Nudie circus clown.

Loop-the-loop until we're dizzy,

Rudie Nudie all fall down!

Rudie Nudie through the screen door—

Rudie running everywhere.
Rudie Nudie round the garden,

and a tickly under there!

Rudie Nudie, Mummy's calling,
'Rudie Nudie, getting cold?'

Rudie run up for a cuddle,
kiss and hug and squeeze and hold.

Rudie Nudie,
pull on jarmies.

Rudie Nudie, time for bed.

But no longer Rudie Nudie—
no...

we're snuggled up instead!

Night, night.